The Closet Gorilla

by Frances Ward Weller

illustrated by Cat Bowman Smith

Macmillan Publishing Company   New York
Collier Macmillan Canada   Toronto
Maxwell Macmillan International Publishing Group
New York   Oxford   Singapore   Sydney

First edition   Printed in Hong Kong.
1 2 3 4 5 6 7 8 9 10

The text of this book is set in 14 point Weidemann Medium. The illustrations are rendered in pen-and-ink and watercolor.

Library of Congress Cataloging-in-Publication Data • Weller, Frances Ward. The closet gorilla / by Frances Ward Weller ; illustrated by Cat Bowman Smith. — 1st ed.   p.   cm.   Summary: Uncle Hugo comes to the rescue on Halloween when Ben needs a gorilla to complete his Tarzan costume. ISBN 0-02-792531-5   [1. Halloween—Fiction. 2. Uncles—Fiction.] I. Smith, Cat Bowman, ill. II. Title. PZ7.W454Cl   1991   [E]—dc20   90-40350   CIP   AC

For my daughter
Alison,
resident critic and treasured friend,
who once upon a Halloween
went roving with the "real" gorilla
—F.W.W.

For Ben S., who will one day have a
gorilla suit of his own.
—C.B.S.

October sunshine puddled the floor, announcing morning, but Ben dived back beneath his sheepskin to escape the day. It was Halloween, and he had a big problem: he needed an ape by five o'clock at the very latest.

He was going to be Tarzan. He would wrap himself in the
sheepskin he pulled over him on drafty nights. He would wear his
leopard-spotted bathing suit and carry his rubber dagger. But to
prove he was Tarzan, he had to have an ape.

"One middle-size brown chimpanzee would do," he'd told his mother. "Like the one at Roy's Toys."

"No way, Ben. Your grandma taught me half the fun of Halloween is using your imagination with whatever's in the closet. You could use Anna's monkey."

But a white plush monkey with a pink nose and strained carrots on one ear was not an ape. Ben was sure you would never catch the real Tarzan with a fuzzy white monkey.

"You could wear a sign," Ben's father said at breakfast.

"Balderdash," Ben whispered to himself. He liked the sound
of Uncle Hugo's word for nonsense; and a sign was nonsense. The
real Tarzan was so strong, quick, and awesome that anyone with
any sense would know him anywhere. And those big pesty kids
who called Ben Pipsqueak, Shrimp, and Little Creep would hoot
louder than ever if he wore a sign. So Ben just sat and glared
at his banana.

It reminded him of Uncle Hugo's closet, with the carnival hat
that dripped kiwis, kumquats, and bananas. Uncle Hugo was an
actor. He knew Shakespeare by heart, and he shaved on TV. He
was serious about make-believe. He was a person you could count
on. "Mom," said Ben, "I need to talk to Uncle Hugo."

"I bet he's still asleep," Ben's mother said, but she dialed anyway.

"I'll call you back when I wake up, Ben," Uncle Hugo mumbled.

"Uncle Hugo," Ben said, "this is serious. I'm going to be Tarzan and I need an ape."

"Serious. Balderdash!" Now Uncle Hugo sounded more awake. "Buy a stuffed chimp."

"Mom says I have to use my head and what's in closets."

"Ah. Pop Anna in that brown bear suit she sleeps in, and make her a mask from a grocery bag."

"She'd cry for sure, or else chew up the bag," Ben grumbled. "Could you come over later and help me with my costume?"

"Ben, I can't," said Uncle Hugo. "I'm filming a banana commercial. But something will turn up. You'll be the greatest Tarzan ever!"

That afternoon they carved the jack-o'-lantern. The pumpkin's smile grew wider and wider, and Ben felt more and more gloomy. As he put on his leopard-spotted bathing suit and lit the jack-o'-lantern, he wished he'd gotten chicken pox for Halloween.

By the time he headed down the dusky driveway with his mother and Anna's white monkey, he wished he'd stayed in bed and slept till Christmas.

Just when he was feeling gloomiest, a tall, thick shadow sprang
from the bushy thicket at the end of the driveway. Ben grabbed
for his mother's hand and his knees turned to jelly, for what stood
under the streetlight was a huge gorilla.

It was covered with shaggy black hair. It had evil-looking, beady eyes. It did a shuffly turn, looking back at Ben as if to be admired. And most astonishing of all was the sign pinned to the thick fur on the gorilla's back. The sign said TARZAN'S APE.

"Ben," said his mother gently, "I think he wants to go with you."

Ben's knees shook.

"And," said his mother, "that's surely all the ape you need!"

Ben took a closer look. The gorilla cocked his head in a way
that seemed a bit familiar. Mom was smiling. And it would be a
big relief to get rid of Anna's white plush monkey.

"Okay," said Ben. "But his sign has got to go."

So they scuffed through the Halloween dark, Ben and his
seven-foot gorilla. The sidewalk was a river of whispery leaves.
Jungly shadows made it even stranger. The Jensens' famous
haunted-house tape boomed from their open attic window.
"Heh-heh-heh." Chains rattled. "Now I've got you, my pretty,"
cackled a creaky voice.

The gorilla didn't say much, but he acted friendly. He let Ben hold his hand and steer him round fireplugs and shrubbery. "It's hard to see in here," he mumbled once in a muffled voice. And later on, "It's also hot. And scratchy."

At every house the door was opened with a startled cry:
"Come see what's here! . . . You won't believe this! . . . Mercy!"
But the gorilla's manners were outstanding. Thanks to his
sweeping bows and stagy waves, each doorway soon was filled
with laughing faces.

At last Ben's sack of treats grew heavy, and the near-November
wind crept underneath his sheepskin. "Come on, Gorilla,"
Ben said. "Let's go home."

Ben's front gate was in sight when whispers sounded on the other side of the Conleys' hedge.

"It's him, the Pipsqueak!"

"You can't tell from here, Paulie; and look what's with him!"

"Joey, it's just some kid on stilts," Paulie hissed back.

Rats. The big kids, after him again. Ben stopped short in a leafy rustle, but the gorilla shuffled onward.

"Grrrrr," said the gorilla softly.

Two more shadows fell across the walkway, one long
and skinny, one short and squat.

"It's Pipsqueak, all right," sang Paulie.

"We could use a little of your candy, Mr. Universe,"
Joey added.

"GRrrrr," said the gorilla.

The real Tarzan would not blush and blubber, Ben was sure.
And anyway, there was a lot of comfort in being with a seven-foot
gorilla. "Balderdash," Ben said bravely. "I'm Tarzan, and
this is my main ape."

"GRRrrrrr," growled the gorilla, more deep and rattly
than before.

Joey and Paulie backed up a little. The gorilla's horrible plastic eyes glinted under the streetlight. "Aw, that's not a real g-gorilla," muttered Paulie.

"GRRRRRRRrrrrr!" With
a real roar the gorilla tossed his
head and waved his hairy arms.

"YEOW!" Joey and Paulie backed up a lot, and then they turned and ran.

The gorilla made suspicious chuckling noises, and Ben laughed aloud. He felt strong, quick, and even a little awesome. "Thanks for a great Halloween," he cried, hugging the gorilla's tummy.

"Balderdash," boomed the gorilla in a growly voice. "Most fun I've had since I wore my Dracula costume to visit Great-aunt Hazel!"

"Next Halloween . . ." But just as Ben began, the gorilla pounced back into the shrubbery. And from the blackest bush Ben heard a growly murmur: "I'll see what else is in my closet!"

"I knew," Ben whispered to himself as he raced a flight of leaves to his own back door, "I just knew I could count on Uncle Hugo!"